50p

THE MONSTERS AT NO. 13

TAKE OFF WITH A KITE!

This lively series is designed for children who have developed reading fluency and enjoy reading complete books on their own.

The stories are attractively presented with plenty of illustrations which make them satisfying and fun! A perfect follow-on from the Read Alone series.

GYLES BRANDRETH

THE MONSTERS AT NO. 13

ILLUSTRATED BY SALLY ROBSON

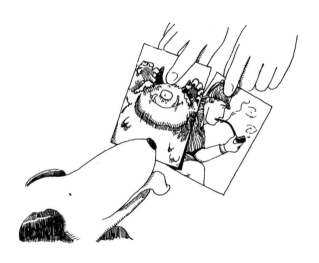

VIKING

VIKING

Published by the Penguin Group
Penguin Books Ltd, 27 Wrights Lane, London W8 5TZ, England
Penguin Books USA Inc., 375 Hudson Street, New York, New York 10014, USA
Penguin Books Australia Ltd, Ringwood, Victoria, Australia
Penguin Books Canada Ltd, 10 Alcorn Avenue, Toronto, Ontario, Canada M4V 3B2
Penguin Books (NZ) Ltd, 182–190 Wairau Road, Auckland 10, New Zealand

Penguin Books Ltd, Registered Offices: Harmondsworth, Middlesex, England

First published 1996
10 9 8 7 6 5 4 3 2 1

Filmset in Linotron Palatino 14/22 pt by
Rowland Phototypesetting Ltd, Bury St Edmunds, Suffolk
Printed in Great Britain by
Butler & Tanner Ltd, Frome and London

A CIP catalogue record for this book is available from the British Library

ISBN 0–670–86341–6

1. Rat-tat-tat

Hamlet Orlando Julius Caesar Brown had a problem. And it wasn't his name. It was the rat-tat-tat at the front door. It was a loud rat-tat-tat. It was a fierce rat-tat-tat. And it seemed to be getting louder and fiercer by the minute. Hamlet hid his head under the pillow.

Hamlet was nine years old and lived at No. 13 Irving Terrace, Hammersmith, West London. It was the first day of the summer holiday and Hamlet didn't want to get out of bed. He certainly didn't want to get out of bed to answer the front door. It would only be the postman and the postman never had any letters for Hamlet.

Rat-tat-tat. The banging was getting worse. Why didn't someone answer?

Where was Mum? Where was Dad?
Where was Susan? Then he remembered.
Mum and Dad were both at work. But
what about Susan? What's the point in
having an older sister, especially a clever-
clogs know-it-all older sister like Susan, if
she doesn't answer the front door when
you need her to?

Hamlet threw his pillow on to the floor
and got out of bed. Rat-tat-tat. "Coming!"
he shouted in a very cross voice.
He went out on to the landing and
marched over to Susan's bedroom. There

THIS ROOM BELON
SUSAN BROWN
DO NOT ENTER
ESPECIALLY IF YOU ARE CAL
HAMLET BROWN

was a large notice pinned to the door. It said:

THIS ROOM BELONGS TO

SUSAN BROWN

DO NOT ENTER

ESPECIALLY IF YOU ARE CALLED

HAMLET BROWN

Hamlet ignored the notice. He yanked open the door and walked in. Susan's room was always so beautifully neat and tidy it made Hamlet feel sick. He expected to find his goodie-goodie eleven-year-old sister sitting quietly at her desk working on one of her school projects. Susan was always working on a project and her projects were always winning prizes at school. At the end of term assembly Mrs Norgate, the headteacher, had declared that "Susan

Brown is a real credit to the school" and had asked everyone to clap while Susan went up to collect a silver cup.

Everybody did clap, except for Hamlet.

Rat-tat-tat. "Coming!" called Hamlet, going out on to the landing again. As he passed the bathroom door he heard the sound of running water. That's where she is, he thought, having another bath. She's always having a bath. Baths are stupid. Susan's stupid. Hamlet banged on the bathroom door.

"What is it?" shouted Susan, who sounded as if she had her head under the shower.

"There's someone at the front door," shouted Hamlet.

"I can't hear you. I'm washing my hair."

Rat-tat-TAT. "Coming!" said Hamlet, running down the stairs. "There's no

need to break the door down."

Who could it be? He knew that if it was a stranger he shouldn't answer. But perhaps it wasn't a stranger. Perhaps it was just the postman after all. Or perhaps it was Dad and he had forgotten his key. Dad was always forgetting things. It wouldn't be Mum. She never forgot anything. Perhaps it was Mum's brother, Uncle Eric from New Zealand, turning up out of the blue, on a surprise visit. Perhaps – *rat-tat-TAT!*

It wasn't the postman. There were three letters already lying on the mat. It must be Dad. Hamlet decided to check by taking a quick peep through the letter-box before opening the door. He bent forward and lifted the flap.

What he saw made his blood run cold and his mouth turn so dry that he couldn't let out a scream even though he wanted to. Staring in through the letter-box was a single, gigantic eye. It was enormous, bulging, bright orange and criss-crossed with horrible dark green veins.

Hamlet let go of the flap and raced up the stairs as fast as his shaking legs would carry him. He rushed straight across the landing into Susan's bedroom. If you stood right at one side of the bedroom window and pressed your face hard against the pane, you could just see the little patch of path that led the few feet from the front gate to the front door of No. 13.

Hamlet could hardly believe his eyes.

His hands began to shake and the top of his head began to tingle. There, standing on the doorstep at No. 13 Irving Terrace, Hammersmith, West London, was an enormous one-eyed monster. It was covered with deep blue and dark grey scales, like a huge fish standing upright, with short legs and long arms. Under the creature's bulging bright orange eye were two dark holes which must have been its nose and, under that, a great grinning mouth that looked as if it could swallow a nine-year-old with a single gulp. Hamlet was sure the monster must have

gigantic teeth, dangerous and sharp, but all he could see was a large, thick, floppy, dark pink tongue.

"It's horrible!" Hamlet shuddered. "And it's seen me!" The monster was looking straight up at Susan's bedroom window. With his left paw he seemed to be waving. With his right paw he was knocking on the front door. "He's come to get me," thought Hamlet. "He's going to break the door down."

Hamlet ran out on to the landing. There was music coming from the bathroom. Hamlet banged on the door.

"Go away!" shouted Susan.

"There's a monster at the door!" bellowed Hamlet.

"I can't hear you. I'm in the bath!"

RAT-TAT-TAT! The beating on the front door was louder than ever. As Hamlet ran down the stairs he saw the

16

monster's horrible grey-green paw
rattling at the letter-box.

Hamlet was only nine. He wasn't
clever like his sister. He wasn't top of his
class (he wasn't quite bottom either), but
he was brave. He ran straight into the
kitchen and quickly looked around. "I'll
use the table," he thought. He didn't
stop to clear the breakfast things off it.
He simply got hold of one end and began
to drag the table towards the hallway. He
just managed to squeeze it through the
kitchen doorway and then he wedged it
as hard as he could against the inside of
the front door. RAT-TAT-TAT.

Hamlet ran back into the kitchen.
Puddles, the Brown family's pet beagle,
was fast asleep in his basket. He snuffled
happily in his sleep. "Fat lot of use you
are as a guard dog," thought Hamlet, as
he picked up one of the kitchen chairs

and marched boldly back to the barricaded front door.

He was just piling a third chair on top of the table and beginning to feel a little bit safer when a voice on the stairs made him jump.

"Hamlet, what are you doing?"

It was Susan. She was standing half-way down the stairs, wrapped from top to toe in one of Mrs Brown's big fluffy bath towels.

"There's a monster at the front door," gasped her brother.

"Oh, good," said Susan.

"What do you mean, 'Oh, good'?" hissed Hamlet.

"I mean," said Susan in her most sensible and matter-of-fact voice, "oh, good, it must be the Munchie Monster. We're expecting him. You'd better let him in."

2. Meet Munchie

Three minutes later, when the chairs and the table had been dragged back to the kitchen, Susan Brown opened the front door with a flourish and said, "Hamlet, meet Munchie!"

Hamlet, who didn't have the first idea what was going on, stepped back in alarm as the huge one-eyed monster stepped over the threshold of No. 13 Irving Terrace.

"Hi, everybody! Good to see you!" The monster had a voice. And to Hamlet's amazement it sounded like a jolly, friendly sort of voice.

"Is this the hippy-hoppy-happy Brown household?" gurgled the monster.

"It certainly is," said Susan, putting out her hand to shake the monster's paw.

"Who is he?" Hamlet whispered to his sister.

"He's Munchie," said Susan.

"Everyone knows Munchie," said the monster with a chuckle.

"I don't," said Hamlet.

"Well, allow me to introduce myself then," said the monster with a bow. "I'm Munchie, the Crunchie-Munchie Cheesy Corn Puff Monster."

When Hamlet had first seen the monster he couldn't believe his eyes. Now he couldn't believe his ears. "Sorry. Who did you say you are?"

"Munchie, the Crunchie-Munchie Cheesy Corn Puff Monster," repeated the monster happily.

"You know Munchie," said Susan. "You must have seen him on TV in the Crunchie-Munchie Corn Puff advertisements."

Hamlet watched a lot of television. Mrs Brown said Hamlet did very little else. But Hamlet couldn't remember seeing this particular monster before.

"What's he doing here?" asked Hamlet.

"He's brought Dad's prize," said Susan. "The Crunchie-Munchie people telephoned to say he'd be arriving at ten o'clock."

"What prize?" asked Hamlet, who was getting more confused by the minute.

"This prize," said the monster, nipping out of the front door and returning a moment later with a gigantic

cardboard box. "A year's supply of delicious cheese-flavoured Crunchie-Munchie Corn Puffs. You'll find three hundred and sixty-five packets in here, one for every day of the year. I packed them myself."

"Thank you," said Susan, as the monster deposited the enormous box on the doormat.

"Well," said the monster, "I'd better be on my way now. I'm glad I found you in after all. For a moment I thought I'd come on the wrong day."

"Excuse me," said Hamlet. "Before you go, do you mind if I take a photograph of you?"

"Delighted," said the monster, immediately striking a monster-like pose in the doorway.

Hamlet ran up to his room and fetched his camera. He only had four pictures left on his film. He used one of them to take a close-up of the extraordinary one-eyed monster standing in the hallway at No. 13 Irving Terrace.

"Now what do you say?" asked the monster.

"Thanks a bunch, Munch!" said Susan.

"That's it," said the monster with a laugh. "'Bye now." And with a cheery wave the great grey-green creature lumbered off.

Hamlet and Susan watched him walk down the road and climb into a bright yellow van. There was a picture of the monster on the side of the van and in large red letters were the words: "CRUNCHIE-MUNCHIE CORN PUFF SNACKS – THEY'RE MONSTROUSLY TASTY!"

"Was it really a man in a costume?" asked Hamlet, scratching his head, when

he and Susan were back in the kitchen
and unpacking the enormous cardboard
box.

"What do you think?" said Susan.

"And why did he bring us all these
packets of corn puffs?"

"Because Dad entered a competition.
He's always going in for competitions on
the sides of packets. Only this time he
won a prize."

Rat-tat-tat.

The knock on the door made Hamlet
jump. Susan laughed. Puddles snuffled
in his basket.

"That'll be Dad," said Susan. "I bet

he's forgotten his key."

"We'd better check," said Hamlet, who thought there might be another monster at the door. Rat-tat-tat.

"Coming!" shouted Susan.

"Hold on," said Hamlet. "I'm bringing Puddles." Hamlet went over to the beagle's basket. Puddles woke up with a start. "Come on, dog," said Hamlet. Puddles padded out into the hallway with Hamlet and Susan.

Rat-tat-tat.

Hamlet bent down to lift the flap on the letter-box. As he lifted it, from the other side of the door came a terrifying sound. It was a loud, fierce, barking noise, like the cry of a wild dog, followed at once by a terrifying high-pitched howl.

"It's another monster!" shrieked Hamlet as he and Susan and Puddles raced one another to the top of the stairs.

They ran into Susan's bedroom and, with their hearts thumping, crept up to the window and peered out.

It wasn't a monster. At least, it didn't look like a monster. It was a man, but clearly it was no ordinary man. He was wearing an old-fashioned cloak, made of tweed, with buttons up the front. On his head was an odd-shaped hat. It looked a bit like a skiing cap. It had a peak at the front and a peak at the back and ear-flaps tied together at the top with a tiny bow. The children couldn't see the man's face, but he seemed to be smoking a funny-looking pipe.

Rat-tat-tat.

"Who do you think it is?" whispered Hamlet.

"I think," Susan said very slowly, "I – think – it's someone called – Sherlock Holmes."

3. The Great Detective

"Do you mean Sherlock Holmes, the famous detective?" asked Hamlet. "*That* Sherlock Holmes?"

"Yes," said Susan. "*That* Sherlock Holmes."

"But what's he doing at our front door?"

"We'd better go and ask him," said Susan, leading the way out of her room and back down the stairs.

"Woof!" yapped Puddles, who didn't know anything about Sherlock Holmes, but did know that he didn't like the sound of the horrible animal the great detective appeared to have brought with him. "Woof! Woof!"

"Don't worry, Puddles," said Susan. "We won't let him in till we know what

he wants." She knelt down on the mat
and lifted the flap.

"Be careful," whispered Hamlet.
Puddles growled.

Susan peered through the letter-box.
All she could see was the man's tweed
cloak. "Excuse me," she said. "Who are
you?"

"My name is Mr Sherlock Holmes,"
said the man in a loud, grand voice. "I

am the world's most famous detective."

"No, you're not!" said Susan, laughing and getting to her feet.

"Yes, I am," protested the voice on the other side of the door.

"No, you're not," repeated Susan as she flung open the front door of No. 13. "You're my dad!"

"So I am!" exclaimed Mr Brown, taking off his hat and stepping into the hallway. "I'm sorry my disguise didn't fool you."

"It fooled Puddles," said Hamlet, who didn't like to admit that it had fooled him too.

"I expect this is what fooled Puddles," said Mr Brown, tapping the portable tape recorder he had tucked underneath his arm.

"What is it?" asked Hamlet.

"It is my latest recording," said Mr

Brown proudly. "A dramatic reading of the terrifying tale of *Sherlock Holmes and the Hound of the Baskervilles*, complete with spooky sound effects."

Mr Brown was an actor, which is how Hamlet came to be called Hamlet Orlando Julius Caesar Brown. They were the names of three of the characters Mr Brown had played in the year Hamlet was born. If Hamlet had been born this year he might have been called Sherlock.

(Or Sherlock Buttons Brown, because Mr
Brown had also played the part of
Buttons in a pantomime at Christmas.)
Mrs Brown was an actor too. She had
played the part of Princess
Badroulboudour in the year Susan was
born, but Mrs Brown wanted her
daughter to have a sensible name and
Susan is a lot easier to spell than
Badroulboudour. Puddles was called
Puddles because when he was a puppy
he made them – lots of them – all over
the place.

Mr Brown was an actor who really
loved acting. In a way, he was acting all
the time, even when he wasn't on a stage
or in a recording studio. Mr Brown also
liked dressing up.

"Shall I take a photo of you in your
costume?" suggested Hamlet.

"Yes, please," said Mr Brown, who

always enjoyed having his photograph taken. "I had hoped they would take a photo of me at the recording studio, but they didn't. I thought a portrait of your father as Sherlock Holmes would look rather good on the cover of the tape. They thought a full-colour picture of the terrifying Hound of the Baskervilles would sell more copies. They're probably right."

"Who is the Hound of the Basker-

villes?" asked Hamlet when he had finished taking Mr Brown's photograph. "Is he a monster?"

"Sort of," said Mr Brown. "Listen to the story and you'll find out."

"Hamlet's got monsters on the brain," said Susan. "It's because the Crunchie-Munchie Monster came."

"Oh, good," said Mr Brown. "Did he bring my prize?"

Susan and Hamlet showed their father the enormous cardboard box filled with corn puff snacks.

"Tuck in," said Mr Brown, handing each of his children a packet and opening a third one for himself and Puddles to share.

"What did you do to win the prize, Dad?" asked Hamlet.

"My boy," said Mr Brown, puffing his chest out with pride, "I sent in ten empty

Crunchie-Munchie Cheesy Corn Puff packets with a slogan of no more than fifteen words explaining why Crunchie-Munchie Cheesy Corn Puffs are my favourite snack food."

"What was your slogan?" asked Susan.

"It was this," said Mr Brown, standing up in the middle of the kitchen and spreading his arms wide. "They're crunchy, they're munchy, they're punchy. I love them for breakfast, tea and lunchy!"

Hamlet and Susan clapped as Mr Brown took a big bow and Puddles sat up and begged for more.

"Sorry, old boy," said Mr Brown patting Puddles on the nose. "No more snacking now. The Browns are going shopping."

"Woof!" yapped Puddles, wagging his tail.

"I'm afraid you can't come," explained Mr Brown. "We're going to the new supermarket over the bridge and there's a big sign in the window that says: 'NO DOGS ALLOWED.' You stay here and guard the house. We won't be long."

In fact, when Mr Brown and Hamlet and Susan reached the new supermarket, the only sign they could see in the window said: "COME ON IN! THOUSANDS OF BARGAINS ON OFFER!! HUNDREDS OF PRIZES TO BE WON!!!"

"I like the sound of that," said Mr Brown, sweeping through the automatic doors.

"We mustn't get anything that isn't on Mum's list," said Susan, very sensibly.

"Quite right," said her father. Fortunately there were bargains to be had and prizes to be won on quite a few of the items on the Brown shopping list, so when, half an hour later, they set off again for home, their six carrier-bags

contained eleven special offers and three
"super new competitions", including one
for Honey Bear Cornflakes which
promised "100 family trips to the world-
famous Teddy Bear Museum in Stratford-
upon-Avon".

"What do we have to do?" asked Mr
Brown.

"Think of an original teddy bear joke,"
said Susan.

"Easy," said Mr Brown. "How do you
start a teddy bear race?"

"Ready, teddy, go!" said Hamlet.

"That's not original," said Susan.

"This is," said Mr Brown. "What's
furry, cuddly and has ten legs?"

"I don't know," said Hamlet and
Susan at the same time.

"Five teddy bears!" said Mr Brown
with a laugh.

Hamlet and Susan laughed too, even

though Mr Brown's joke wasn't a very funny one.

"What doesn't growl but sounds like a bear?" asked Mr Brown.

"Stop!" exclaimed Hamlet.

"That isn't the answer," said Mr Brown.

"No, stop, look!" said Hamlet, hurriedly putting down the carrier-bags he was holding and pulling his camera out of his anorak pocket. "Look in the river."

The Browns were half-way across Hammersmith Bridge. "Over there," said Hamlet, pointing down river. "It's a gigantic sea monster."

"Oh, my goodness," said Mr Brown, peering over the side of the bridge, "so it is!"

4. The Monster from the Deep

"It can't be a sea monster," said Susan, trying to be helpful. "This isn't the sea, after all. This is the River Thames."

"Don't be such a know-all," said Hamlet, leaning over the rail of the bridge to take a photograph. "Whatever it is it's definitely a monster."

"It looks more like an enormous serpent to me," said Mr Brown.

"I can't see it," said Susan.

"There, stupid!" said Hamlet, jabbing his finger out towards the middle of the river. "There!"

"Where?"

"It's disappeared," said Mr Brown. And it had. Whatever it was had vanished into the muddy grey water. A river police launch rushed past.

"The boat's frightened it away," said Hamlet.

"You're imagining things," said Susan.

"I saw something," said Mr Brown.

"And I took a photograph of it," said Hamlet with satisfaction.

The Browns didn't talk much as they walked back to No. 13 Irving Terrace with their shopping. Mr Brown and Hamlet were thinking about the strange creature they had seen swimming below the bridge. Susan was busy planning her next project. She was trying to remember

if it was Mercury or Venus that was nearest to the sun. She decided it was Mercury.

When they got home, Hamlet and Susan unpacked the shopping while Mr Brown made a pot of tea and Puddles ate another packet of Crunchie-Munchie Corn Puffs.

"Do you know what?" said Mr Brown all of a sudden. "I think I've cracked it. That serpent is the Loch Ness monster!"

"What's it doing under Hammersmith Bridge?" asked Susan, who didn't believe it was a monster at all.

"It's lost," said Mr Brown. "Or it's on its summer holidays. Anyway, it's swum down from Scotland and we've seen it."

"You've seen it," said Susan firmly.

"I've photographed it," said Hamlet and, for no good reason, he stuck his tongue out at his sister.

Susan pretended not to notice and went off to her bedroom to collect her giant encyclopaedia. She had been presented with it at school when she won the prize for her project on the human body. She brought it back to the kitchen and began leafing through the pages.

"Lizard, llama, lobster – here we are," she said. "'Loch Ness monster. For nearly six hundred years sightings have been reported of a strange creature in the land-locked lake of Loch Ness in the Highlands of Scotland.' If the lake is land-locked nothing can swim out."

"Perhaps it can fly," suggested Hamlet.

"It didn't look like a flying monster to me," said Mr Brown, shaking his head sadly.

"Did it look like this?" asked Susan,

holding up the book and showing her father and brother the drawing in the encyclopaedia.

"Yes!" exclaimed Hamlet with a cheer. "I didn't see the head or the neck, but I certainly saw those two humps on the back. You'll see them in my photograph."

"Yes, indeed," said Mr Brown, looking closely at the picture in the book. "That's our monster from the deep all right."

Rat-tat-tat.

"And that," said Mr Brown happily,

moving towards the front door, "will be
your wonderful mother and my darling
wife."

"Check first, Dad," said Hamlet
quickly.

"No need," said Mr Brown, "I'd
recognize that rat-tat-tat anywhere." He
flung open the front door, made an
elegant bow and said, "Welcome home,
my sweet. You are looking lovelier than
ever!"

The ginger-headed policeman on the
doorstep tugged at his moustache,
coughed and said, "Excuse me, sir, but
have you been drinking?"

"No, Officer," stammered Mr Brown.
"I mean yes, Officer, but only tea. You
see, it's a case of mistaken identity. I was
expecting my wife, but she doesn't look
anything like you."

"And would your wife be a Mrs Brown

of No. 13 Irving Terrace, Hammersmith, West London?''

"She would indeed, Officer," said Mr Brown proudly.

"Where is she?" said Susan.

"Is she all right?" said Hamlet. The children had joined their father at the front door and were now looking up anxiously at the ginger-headed policeman.

"She's very well," he said slowly, tugging again at his droopy red moustache. "It's not how she is that's bothering us. It's where she is."

"And where is she?" asked Mr Brown in a state of some alarm.

"Believe it or not, sir," said the policeman, "she is in an old churchyard not five hundred yards from where we're standing now."

"In a churchyard?" squealed Hamlet, who had seen a ghost as well as a monster in his time.

"She's quite safe," explained the policeman.

"What's she doing?" asked Mr Brown, wide-eyed with amazement.

"She's sitting cross-legged on top of a tombstone. And she says she won't move."

"What's it all about?" said Mr Brown.

"Don't ask me," said the policeman, giving his moustache another tug. "You'd better ask her."

5. The Famous Actress

Five minutes later, Mr Brown and Hamlet and Susan and Puddles and the ginger-headed policeman were standing in the middle of a tiny churchyard just a stone's throw from Hammersmith Bridge.

Strictly speaking, it wasn't a churchyard any longer. The old church had been bombed during the Second World War and an ugly-looking factory building, with a flat roof and no windows, had been put up in its place. The churchyard itself wasn't used any more. It was small and untidy, with broken bottles and empty cans scattered everywhere and old newspapers blowing about in the wind.

The little path leading from the rusty iron gate was overgrown with weeds and so were the graves. There were only eight of them. On the smallest and newest (and it wasn't very new: if you looked carefully you could see the year 1937 on the tombstone) sat a jam jar filled with dead flowers. On the largest and oldest (it was really quite large and exactly two hundred years old) sat Mrs Brown. She had her legs crossed and her arms folded and, sitting there, she looked like an odd sort of living statue.

"Hi, gang!" she said cheerfully, as her family and the ginger-headed policeman made their way up the path.

"Hi, Mum," said Hamlet and Susan, who weren't sure what else to say. They were used to Mr Brown doing funny things, but Mrs Brown was usually very sensible.

"It's good to see you," said Mrs Brown. "But why is your father dressed up as Sherlock Holmes?"

"Is that who he's supposed to be?" muttered the policeman, pulling on his moustache.

"More to the point," said Mr Brown to his wife, "what on earth are you doing sitting on this tombstone?"

"That's easily explained," said Mrs Brown, with a smile. "It's a protest."

"A protest about what?" asked Hamlet.

"A protest about that!" said Mrs Brown pointing to a large "FOR SALE" notice that was tied to the railings at one corner of the churchyard. "The Council want to sell the churchyard. And they mustn't be allowed to."

"Why not?" asked Mr Brown.

"Because Mrs Brown is buried here."

"Who's Mrs Brown?" asked Mr Brown.

"I thought Mrs Brown was your wife," said the policeman, pulling a notebook and pencil out of his top pocket.

"She is!" protested Mr Brown, who was now almost as confused as the unhappy constable.

"I'm talking about Mrs Isabella Brown, the famous actress," explained Mrs Brown. "This is her tombstone. She's buried here. Read what it says."

Susan leant over and read the words

that were carved into the side of the
tomb. "Here lies Mrs Isabella Brown,
Actress, 1735–1800."

"I've never heard of her," said Mr
Brown.

"You would have done if you had
been alive two hundred years ago," said
Mrs Brown. "She played all the great
parts. She was in the first production of
Beauty and the Beast."

"Isn't that a story about a monster?" asked Hamlet.

"Yes," said Mrs Brown. "It's about a monster who falls in love with a beautiful princess. Mrs Brown was very beautiful."

"And you are very beautiful too, my dear," said Mr Brown, "but you can't sit out here all night."

"I can and I will," protested Mrs Brown.

"You can't and you won't," said the ginger-headed policeman fiercely. "This is Council property."

"It may be Council property now," said Mrs Brown, "but once upon a time it was a lovely little churchyard and a very special person is buried here."

"Mum's right," said Susan.

"She usually is," said Mr Brown, with a smile.

"Don't you see," continued Mrs
Brown, "this is a small piece of theatrical
history. We're actors and, by a funny
coincidence, we've got the same name as
Mrs Brown. We ought to save the
churchyard where she's buried if we
can."

"I suppose we could always try to buy
it ourselves," suggested Mr Brown,
trying to be helpful. "How much is it?"

"Ten thousand pounds," said the policeman.

"Ten thousand pounds!" exclaimed Mr Brown. "It can't be. Ten thousand pounds for a patch of ground no bigger than a pocket handkerchief. It's daylight robbery!"

"Don't blame me," said the policeman, scratching his moustache with his pencil. "Blame the Council. They want to build two garages here."

Mrs Brown almost burst into tears. "Two horrid garages," she gasped, "for two horrid, smelly cars. We can't let it happen."

"We won't let it happen," said Mr Brown firmly. "We'll think of something." And they did.

6. Monsters on the Brain

That evening the Brown family sat around the kitchen table at No. 13 Irving Terrace deciding what to do.

"We need a plan," said Mr Brown.

"We need ten thousand pounds," said Mrs Brown.

"Woof!" said Puddles, which meant: "I need more supper so now I've eaten my tin of dog food, please can I have another packet of Crunchie-Munchie Cheesy Corn Puff snacks?"

Hamlet opened up another of Mr Brown's prize packets of corn puffs and Susan opened up her encyclopaedia. There were lots of famous Browns in the book. There was a gardener and a doctor and a painter and an aviator who had taken part in the first non-stop aeroplane flight across the Atlantic.

"We Browns have always been high flyers," said Mr Brown with a chuckle. Mrs Brown wasn't really in the mood for Mr Brown's jokes. "Is Mrs Brown there?" she asked.

"Yes, she is," said Susan triumphantly. "Listen to this: 'Mrs Isabella Brown, London-born actress and favourite of King Charles II, celebrated

BROWN
MRS ISABELLA
BROWN, LOND
ACTRESS AND FA
OF KING CH
CELEBRATED
'N 'BEA

for playing Beauty in *Beauty and the Beast*
and Juliet in *Romeo and Juliet.*' "

"I told you she was famous," said Mrs
Brown.

"I know a poem about Romeo and
Juliet," said Mr Brown:

"'Twas in a restaurant they met,
Romeo and Juliet.
He had no money to pay the debt,
So Rome' owed what Julie ate!"

Hamlet laughed and Mr Brown took a
bow. Mrs Brown looked cross. "This is
no time for silly poems," she said. "Our
problem is that we've got no money to
pay the Council for the churchyard and if
we don't find ten thousand pounds from
somewhere poor Isabella Brown's
tombstone is going to be turned into a
garage!"

"I know the problem," said Mr Brown

very seriously. "And, my dear," he went on, suddenly beaming from ear to ear, "I know the answer!"

"You do?" said Susan, amazed.

"I do!" said Mr Brown happily and he began to skip around the kitchen in excitement. "By jove, I've cracked it, I've really cracked it!"

"Well?" said Mrs Brown.

"Woof!" said Puddles, who hoped Mr Brown was looking so happy because he had just won another year's supply of Crunchie-Munchie Cheesy Corn Puff snacks.

"This is the plan," said Mr Brown when he had stopped dancing and was sitting down at the kitchen table once more. "Listen carefully. Tomorrow morning we all get up bright and early. We collect our wheelbarrow and our lawnmower, our garden shears and our

58

garden fork, and everything else we
need, and we take them to the
churchyard. What do we do with them
when we get them there? We set to
work! We cut the grass, we weed the
path, we clear away all the rubbish. Then
we come back and collect all the
scrubbing-brushes we can find and we
take them, with buckets and buckets of

hot soapy water, and we scrub and clean those gravestones till they look as good as new.''

''What about the railings?'' said Mrs Brown, who was beginning to get the idea. ''Do we paint the railings?''

''We do indeed,'' said Mr Brown, ''with shiny black paint. And we mend the gate and oil the hinges so they don't

squeak. In short, my dears, we turn that sad little churchyard into the brightest and the best-kept churchyard in the world!"

"Then what?" asked Hamlet, who thought all this gardening and cleaning and painting and mending sounded like an awful lot of work.

"And then," said Mr Brown, leaning forward and lowering his voice as if he was going to tell his family a very important secret, "and then, we open the churchyard to the public – and make them pay to come in. £1 for adults, 50p for children."

"But will enough people want to come?" asked Mrs Brown, who wanted the idea to work but wasn't sure that it would.

"Everybody will want to come!" exclaimed Mr Brown.

"Why will they?" asked Hamlet.

"Because they'll all want to meet Mrs Brown!"

"Mrs Brown!" said Mrs Brown, who was starting to get confused.

"Yes," said Mr Brown, leaning back in his chair and grinning broadly. "Mrs Isabella Brown, the famous actress, will be there in person. And she won't be alone."

"No?" said Mrs Brown, raising an eyebrow.

"Woof!" said Puddles, wagging his tail and hoping that the other person would turn out to be the Crunchie-Munchie Monster.

"No, she won't be alone," said Mr Brown with a wink, "because at her side will be none other than His Majesty King Charles the Second!"

"Do you mean what I think you

mean?'' asked Mrs Brown slowly.

"I do indeed," said Mr Brown, rubbing
his hands together with pleasure. "You
and I, my sweet, are going to dress up as
the ghosts of Good King Charles and the
beautiful Isabella. And young Hamlet
and young Susan here can be their
children."

"I don't think Mrs Brown and the king were married, were they?" said Susan, quickly flicking through the encyclopaedia.

"That's a detail," chortled Mr Brown. "The point is that everyone will want to come. Everybody wants to meet members of the royal family and famous actresses, especially when they're ghosts."

"It might just work," said Mrs Brown with a smile.

"It will work!" said Mr Brown with a chuckle.

"What time do we start?" said Susan with a yawn.

"Early," said Mrs Brown, "which is why you two need to get off to bed now."

"Can I take Dad's Sherlock Holmes tape to listen to in bed?" asked Hamlet.

64

"Of course you can," said Mr Brown, "but it's a spooky story, so don't give yourself nightmares. Goodnight."

"Sweet dreams," said Mrs Brown, as Hamlet and Susan made their way up to bed.

That night Mr Brown dreamt about life at the court of King Charles II and Mrs Brown dreamt about saving the tombstone of Isabella Brown. Susan Brown dreamt about winning a prize for her project on the planets and Hamlet Brown dreamt about monsters and sea-serpents and the horrible howling of the Hound of the Baskervilles.

All of a sudden, at one o'clock in the morning, Hamlet woke up. Rat-tat-tat. Rat-tat-tat. Was it the front door? No, it was the window rattling in the wind. Hamlet sat up. Rat-tat-tat. Rat-tat-tat. He slipped out of bed, tiptoed quietly to the

window, pulled back the curtain and looked out. There was a full moon so that Hamlet could see very clearly, and what he saw sitting on the roof of the old shed at the bottom of the little garden at the back of No. 13 Irving Terrace sent a shiver down his spine. It was the outline of a wild animal. Hamlet had never seen anything like it before. Was it a wolf? Was it a panther? Was it the Hound of the Baskervilles?

Hamlet ran quickly out of his room and across the landing. "Susan, wake up!" he hissed at his sister, who was lying in bed fast asleep.

"What is it?" she said blearily, blinking at Hamlet, as he tugged at her.

"Get up quickly," said Hamlet. "There's something strange in the garden."

"What is it?" asked Susan.

"I don't know. Come and have a look." But when Susan and her brother got back to Hamlet's bedroom window the creature, whatever it was, had disappeared.

"It must have been a dream," said Susan as she went back to her room. "You've got monsters on the brain."

"It wasn't a dream," said Hamlet as he climbed back into bed.

7. "Woof!" said Puddles

The next day was Tuesday, and by seven
o'clock in the morning Mr Brown was up
and dressed and making breakfast in the
kitchen. He fried 4 eggs, grilled 6 rashers
of bacon, buttered 8 slices of toast and
cooked 222 baked beans. (He counted the
eggs, bacon and toast. He guessed at the
number of baked beans.)

"We need a big breakfast because it's a
big day and there's a big job of work to
do."

There was. From 8.30 that morning till
almost eight o'clock on Thursday
evening Mr Brown and Mrs Brown,
Hamlet and Susan didn't stop. They
trundled between No. 13 Irving Terrace
and the little churchyard with their
wheelbarrow and their lawnmower, with

shovels and garden forks, with shears
and scrubbing-brushes, with buckets of
water and pots of paint.

On Tuesday they did the gardening,
clearing away the rubbish, cutting the
grass, reshaping the path, weeding the
graves. On Wednesday they scrubbed
the tombstones. They scrubbed and they
scrubbed until Hamlet said, "I can't
scrub any more!"

Mr Brown said, "Nearly there!" and

Puddles said, "Woof!" which meant "Well done!"

On Thursday Mr and Mrs Brown mended the gate and painted it and oiled the hinges so they didn't squeak, and Hamlet and Susan painted the railings (and bits of each other) with lovely shiny black paint. By mistake, two blobs of paint landed on Puddles's nose. He was very cross, but two packets of corn puffs made him feel a little better.

On Tuesday, Wednesday and Thursday night, the moment the Browns and Puddles clambered into their beds and basket they fell fast asleep. Mr and Mrs Brown and Hamlet and Susan had never worked so hard in all their lives and Puddles was exhausted just watching them.

Each night Hamlet tucked his camera under his pillow. He had just one picture left on his film. He wanted to use it to take a photograph of the strange animal he had seen on the roof of the shed at the bottom of the garden. It hadn't been a dream. He was sure of that.

On Tuesday night the Browns had spaghetti bolognaise for supper and Hamlet slept like a log. On Wednesday night they had fish and chips and Hamlet slept so soundly that Puddles had to jump on his bed and lick his face to wake him up in the morning. On Thursday night Mr Brown cooked cheese on toast with grilled tomatoes and, at one o'clock in the morning, Hamlet woke up.

There was no strange noise, no howling, no barking, no rattling of the window in the wind. Hamlet sat up in bed. He couldn't hear a sound, but he was sure the creature was there. He

reached under the pillow and took hold
of his camera. Quietly he pushed back
the duvet, slipped out of bed and tiptoed
across to the window. He pulled back the
curtain. The moon was clear and bright.

He looked towards the roof of the garden
shed. There was nothing there. He
looked down at the little patch of grass
just below his window. There it was, as
large as life and standing only a few feet
from him. Hamlet took his photograph.

"I'm not dreaming," he thought, "that's for sure."

On Friday morning, first thing, Mr Brown and Hamlet set off for Berman's, the theatrical costumiers in Camden Town. They took Mrs Brown's and Susan's measurements with them. They also took the film from Hamlet's camera and, on the way to the underground station, stopped off at the chemist to get it developed. "Oh, good," said Mr Brown, "there's a special offer. You might win a prize."

While Hamlet and his father were collecting the costumes, Mrs Brown was at home telephoning all the newspapers to tell them about the rather special ghosts who would be appearing that weekend in a little churchyard in Hammersmith, and Susan was sitting at the kitchen table designing a poster:

THIS SATURDAY AND SUNDAY

10.00 a.m. to 6.00 p.m.

in the Churchyard, Burbage Lane,

Hammersmith

FOR THE FIRST TIME IN OVER 200 YEARS

IN PERSON

THE GHOSTS OF

MRS ISABELLA BROWN

(The Famous Actress!)

AND

HIS MAJESTY KING CHARLES II

WITH HIS

KING CHARLES SPANIEL

Adults £1 . . . . Children 50p

Guided Tours . . . . Refreshments

"That's marvellous," said Mrs Brown, admiring the poster when Susan had finished it, "but where on earth are we going to find a King Charles spaniel?"

"Woof!" said Puddles, happily

munching his first corn puff of the day.

After lunch, Mrs Brown and Susan took the poster to the library and photocopied it a hundred times. The photocopying cost £10. "I hope it's worth it," said Mrs Brown.

"This looks interesting," said the librarian. "Can I keep one to pin up on the notice-board?"

That afternoon, Mrs Brown and Susan walked all around Hammersmith. They visited fifty-two shops, twenty-one

offices, seventeen restaurants and nine pubs, and left a poster in each one of them. When they got home their legs ached and their feet were sore.

"Do you think anyone will come?" said Susan.

"Woof!" said Puddles.

Puddles was right. When Mr and Mrs Brown and Hamlet and Susan, all dressed up in their magnificent costumes, arrived at the little churchyard at half-past nine on Saturday morning, the street was already crowded.

"I'm afraid we don't open till ten," said Mr Brown, fighting his way to the front of the queue.

"That's all right, Your Majesty," said a happy voice in the crowd. "We've waited two hundred years for this. Another half hour won't matter."

Hamlet and Susan were stationed by

the shiny black gate to collect the money as the visitors came in. Mrs Brown, dressed as the famous actress in her celebrated role of Beauty in *Beauty and the Beast*, was in charge of the guided tours. Mr Brown, as King Charles II, looked after the refreshments.

As well as showing everyone around the tiny churchyard and feeding them with orange squash and Crunchie-Munchie Cheesy Corn Puffs, the Browns entertained the visitors with a short show that they repeated five times during the day. Mr and Mrs Brown (still dressed as Beauty and King Charles) acted a scene from *Romeo and Juliet*, Susan sang a song about 'Good King Charles's Golden Days', and Hamlet gave an acrobatic display. (Well, he did a cartwheel, three somersaults and stood on his head.)

By the end of Saturday over two hundred people had toured the little churchyard and watched the show. On the Sunday there were even more visitors, including at least five newspaper reporters, a television crew, someone from the local radio station and a photographer from a magazine called *Dogs Today* who had come to take a picture of the King Charles spaniel. "It looks suspiciously like a beagle to me," he muttered as he took the photograph.

"Woof!" said Puddles.

"We've got a hit on our hands!" laughed Mr Brown.

"Woof! Woof!" said Puddles. And he meant it.

8. "Follow Me!"

At breakfast on Monday morning everyone sitting around the kitchen table at No. 13 Irving Terrace, Hammersmith, West London, was happy.

Mr Brown was admiring a photograph of himself in the *Daily Mail*. Hamlet was explaining to Puddles that there were no more Crunchie-Munchie Cheesy Corn Puff snacks because every single packet had been sold as part of the refreshments. Mrs Brown and Susan were counting out all the money for the umpteenth time. "I don't believe it," said Mrs Brown, grinning from ear to ear. "We've made over a thousand pounds."

"One thousand, one hundred and eleven pounds and thirty-two pence, to be precise," said Susan.

"Ten more weekends like this and we'll be able to buy the churchyard!"

"Hooray!" said Mr Brown, picking up another newspaper to see if he was in it.

Rat-tat-tat.

"It's a bit early for visitors," said Mrs Brown.

"Probably a reporter wanting an exclusive interview with King Charles,"

said Mr Brown. "Leave it to me."

"Be careful, Dad," said Hamlet.

"You and your monsters!" said Susan.

Rat-tat-tat.

Mr Brown opened the front door wide. "His Majesty is not yet dressed," he said very grandly.

"It's not His Majesty we've come to see," said the ginger-headed policeman on the doorstep. "It's you."

"I hope nothing's the matter," said Mrs Brown, hurrying anxiously into the hallway.

"Everything's the matter," said the constable, tugging at his droopy red moustache. "This gentleman here is Mr Blurtt from the Council. He will explain."

Mr Blurtt was a small man with small eyes, a small mouth and a very small black moustache. "I have reason to

believe," he said in a horrid, whiny sort
of voice, "that you have been trespassing
on Council property."

"Yes, but – " protested Mrs Brown.

"Kindly do not interrupt," said Mr
Blurtt sharply. "I have reason to believe
that you have been trespassing on
Council property in fancy dress –"

"I can explain," exclaimed Mr Brown.

"Accompanied," continued Mr Blurtt,
raising his voice, "by two children also
dressed in funny clothes and by an ugly-

looking beagle dog apparently pretending to be a King Charles spaniel."

"Woof!" growled Puddles.

"What, may I ask," continued Mr Blurtt, trying to make himself look as tall and important as possible, "is the explanation for this extraordinary behaviour?"

"We were trying to raise ten thousand pounds to save the churchyard," said Mrs Brown.

"So I understand," said Mr Blurtt, with a horrid smile. "And how much did you raise?"

"One thousand, one hundred and eleven pounds and thirty-two pence," said Susan, holding up the enormous plastic bucket that contained all the money.

"That's a start," said Mr Blurtt. "If you let me have the rest of the money, we will overlook the matter of the trespassing and the churchyard is yours."

"What?" said Mr Brown, who couldn't believe what he was hearing.

"You heard me," said Mr Blurtt.

"Oh, Mr Blurtt," said Mrs Brown, "you wonderful little man!" She gave him an enormous hug. "Are you saying that if we give you ten thousand pounds we can definitely have the churchyard?"

"Yes," said Mr Blurtt, with a nod. "Of course, I will need all the money by lunchtime."

"By lunchtime?" exclaimed Mrs Brown.

"That's impossible," said Mr Brown. "Can't you give us a few more weeks?"

"No," said Mr Blurtt. "If you can produce ten thousand pounds by lunchtime the churchyard is yours. If you can't, it will be sold to a very nice man who is coming to see me at two o'clock. He wants to build two garages on the site and I know he's got ten thousand pounds for a fact."

"But – " protested Mr Brown.

"Good day," said Mr Blurtt, with another horrid little smile. "I may see you at lunchtime. You will find me in my office at the Town Hall. Any time up to one o'clock will do."

"I don't believe it," said Mr Brown with a heavy sigh as soon as Mr Blurtt and the ginger-headed policeman had gone.

"I do," said Mrs Brown sadly.

"What are we going to do?" asked Susan.

"I don't know," said Mr Brown.

"I don't know," said Mrs Brown.

"I do," said Hamlet. "Follow me!"

9. The Monster at No. 13

"Where are we going?" panted Mr Brown, as he tried to keep up with Hamlet as he ran down Irving Terrace towards the High Street.

"Over Hammersmith Bridge!" called Hamlet.

"What for?" asked Susan, who could run just as fast as her brother.

"You'll see," shouted Hamlet.

Four minutes later, puffing and panting, the Brown family found themselves outside the new supermarket on the other side of the bridge.

"Here we are," said Hamlet. "Follow me!" Hamlet led the way through the automatic doors into the shop. "This way!" he called, picking up a trolley and marching down the aisle marked

"GROCERIES". Suddenly he stopped. "There!" he said.

"It's a box of teabags," said Mr Brown, who was still very out of breath.

"Exactly," said Hamlet.

"How's a box of teabags going to help save the churchyard, Hamlet?" asked Susan.

"Read what it says on the side of the box," said Hamlet with a smile.

Mrs Brown picked up the box of teabags and read: "TIP-TOP TEA: THE BEST INSTANT CUPPA THERE IS."

"Go on," said Hamlet.

"SUPER INSTANT CASH PRIZE.

WE'RE GIVING AWAY £10,000 – INSTANTLY. TO DISCOVER IF YOU ARE A WINNER LOOK OUT FOR THE MESSAGE INSIDE THE BOX."

"Let's buy the lot!" said Mr Brown.

Ten minutes later, Mr and Mrs Brown, Hamlet and Susan were standing outside the supermarket with 16 carrier-bags containing 244 boxes of Tip-Top Teabags.

"There isn't a moment to lose," said Mr Brown, checking his watch. "We've got to be at the Town Hall in an hour and a half."

It took the Browns almost an hour to open every box. At the bottom of each of the first 243 boxes the message was the same: "SORRY! YOU HAVEN'T WON A PRIZE THIS TIME. BETTER LUCK NEXT TIME!"

"Who's going to open the last box?" asked Dad.

"Hamlet can," said Susan. "It was his idea."

With trembling fingers, Hamlet unwrapped the very last box. "This'll be the one," he said. It wasn't. The message was just the same: "SORRY! YOU HAVEN'T WON A PRIZE THIS TIME. BETTER LUCK NEXT TIME!"

"I'm afraid we've run out of luck," said Mrs Brown sadly, as they trudged home over the bridge. "Poor Isabella Brown."

"Sorry, Mum," said Hamlet.

Going along the High Street towards Irving Terrace they passed the chemist's shop, and Hamlet went in to pick up his photographs.

When they got home, Mr Brown said, "Anyone fancy a cup of tea?"

"No, thank you," said Mrs Brown. "I don't think I'll ever want a cup of tea again."

Hamlet sat at the kitchen table and looked at his photographs. "That's the Crunchie-Munchie Monster," he said, showing the picture to Puddles, who wagged his tail. "And that's Dad dressed as Sherlock Holmes."

"Let me see," said Mr Brown.

"What's this?" asked Susan.

"It's the sea monster," said Hamlet proudly.

"It looks more like two tyres floating in the water to me," said Susan.

"I'm afraid that's what it looks like to me too," said Mr Brown, looking closely at the picture.

"What about this then?" said Hamlet, holding up the last picture for the whole family to look at.

"It's a fox!" exclaimed Mrs Brown. "And in our garden!"

"Isn't it beautiful," said Susan.

Hamlet didn't say anything. He wasn't looking at the pictures any more. He was reading a small piece of paper that was tucked in the back of the packet of photographs. "Listen to this, everybody. 'Congratulations! You have won the Happy Snaps Holiday of a Lifetime – a trip round the world in eighty days. Or you can have the cash prize of £8,888.88! The choice is yours!'"

"Yippee!" shouted Susan as Mr Brown started dancing round the kitchen and Mrs Brown gave her son an enormous hug.

At exactly three minutes to one, Mr and Mrs Brown, Hamlet and Susan ran up the front steps of the Town Hall.

"Well done," said Mr Blurtt. "£1,111.32 plus £8,888.88 makes a grand total of £10,000.20. The churchyard is yours!"

"Thank you!" said the Browns all at once.

"And there's 20p change," said Mr Blurtt. "Who gets that?"

"Puddles," said Hamlet. "He wants to buy a packet of Crunchie-Munchie Cheesy Corn Puffs."

"He's getting fat," said Susan.

"Yes," said Hamlet. "He's the monster at No. 13!"